MAMBI AND THE FOREST FIRE

MAMBI AND THE FOREST FIRE

Nandana Dev Sen

Illustrations by Saskia Pekelharing

PUFFIN BOOKS

PUFFIN BOOKS

USA | Canada | UK | Ireland | Australia
New Zealand | India | South Africa | China

Puffin Books is part of the Penguin Random House group of companies
whose addresses can be found at global.penguinrandomhouse.com

Published by Penguin Random House India Pvt. Ltd
7th Floor, Infinity Tower C, DLF Cyber City,
Gurgaon 122 002, Haryana, India

First published in Puffin by Penguin Books India 2016

10 9 8 7 6 5 4 3 2

ISBN 9780143334125

For sale in the Indian Subcontinent only

Book design by Devangana Dash
Printed at Replika Press Pvt. Ltd, India

www.penguin.co.in

To my Marvellous Monkeys:
CoKo Loco, Eva Diva, Hili Gili Pili, Jassu Passu,
Julia Coolia, Lethal Ethan and Sulo Debi.

Leaping love,
Toom-Monkey

To Jesse and Eli and all the
other monkeys close to my heart,

Saskia

It was a dry and sizzling summer.

Mambi the Monkey lived in a tall mango tree ...

right in the middle of the forest.

Mambi wasn't very big, but she had a very big smile.
She was also quiet, and a bit shy.

When Mambi was excited—which was very often—
her round eyes **sparkled**, and her long tail **swished**
from side to side.

On the highest branch of the same
tree, lived **Koko the Crow.**

Koko loved to chatter away without a stop ...

about all the places she could fly to ...
and how clever her baby birds were going to be!

Koko had laid three pearly blue eggs
with lots of dots and spots on them.
She was going to become Mama Crow any day now!

'I am going to fly with my babies to the end of the world!'
boasted Koko.

'Don't you wish you could FLY like me, Mambi?'

With a great big flutter,
Koko flew from the mango tree to a shady hill,
next to a cool green lake.

Mambi's eyes started
to SHINE.

Mambi tried to fly after her from the same branch, flapping her arms like Koko's wings.

But all she could manage was a big, cartwheeling TUM BLE...

straight into the jasmine bush below!

Koko CACKLED with laughter.

She flew back to the mango tree ...

dancing in the wind.

Mambi watched Koko glide through the sky.

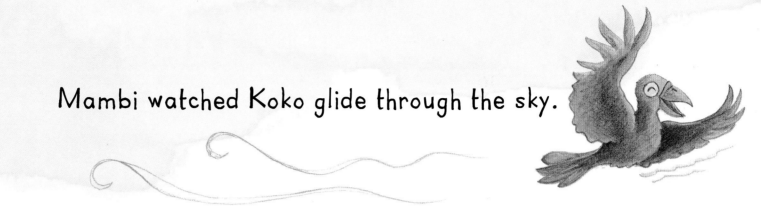

'I wish I had wings,' Mambi said to herself.
'Then I would FLY like Koko!'

Next to the jasmine bush, there was a shallow pond.
It was the home of **Tonga the Turtle.**

Tonga was very handsome.

His big shell had a fine orange pattern,
and always looked smooth and polished.

Tonga never seemed to worry about a thing.

'Isn't it the hottest day ever, Mambi!'

Tonga lazily lifted his head above the water as he swam.

'Care to join me for a dip in the pool?'

Mambi's tail started to TWITCH.

She stepped into the pond on all fours.
But the water sent shivers through her soft brown fur.

She didn't like the feel of it one bit ...

Mambi felt like she couldn't breathe in the water!

Panicking and spluttering,
she jumped back into the jasmine bush.

Tonga CHUCKLED to himself.
He dived into the water,
sending sparkling silver ripples all over the pond.

Mambi watched Tonga sail away,
his orange shell gleaming in the sun.

'I wish I had flippers,' said Mambi to herself.
'Then I would SWIM like Tonga!'

The day got hotter and hotter.
The little pond almost dried up
in the blazing sun.

All the animals
tried to find cool spots
in the forest.

But there were NO shady bits left.

The Deer GROANED in the terrible heat.
And the Parrots SQUAWKED loudly.

Later that day, Koko's eggs hatched.

Three
perfect
little
chicks
were born!

When Koko fed them with her strong dark beak,
her babies opened their mouths wide.

Their little beaks were bright red inside.

'How pretty!' thought Mambi, as she dozed off,
fanning herself with a banana leaf.

As night fell, the whole forest slowly fell asleep.

The Parrot family—which was a big one—
cuddled up together in the banyan tree.

And the Fawn twins curled around Mother and Father Deer.

In the middle of the night, Mambi woke up
with a start, feeling the scorching heat.

The forest was on FIRE!

But Mambi was frightened of water.

She could still feel herself gasping for air in the pond.

'MAMBI!' yelled Tonga again, terrified.

Forgetting her own fear, Mambi LEAPED into the pond.

Quickly, she picked Tonga up in her arms.

Tonga's beautiful shell made him very heavy

for a little monkey to carry.

But even when her tail caught fire,

Mambi did not let Tonga go!

Holding Tonga tightly,
Mambi bounded bravely to the shady hill,
which was safe from the fire.

She placed Tonga,
and her own burning tail,
in the cool green lake.

When she looked up, Mambi was shocked to see that the
mango tree was burning too!

'KOKO!' yelled Mambi.

'You need to fly out of the tree with your babies NOW!'

Mambi was VERY scared.

She didn't know what to do!

She could still feel the sharp sting of the fire burning her tail.

She remembered her big fall from the mango tree earlier.

And how Koko had laughed and laughed as she was falling.

But poor Koko was in tears now.

'HELP!'

she cawed loudly, in total panic.

Mambi JUMPED into the red-hot blaze
without another thought.
She sprang from one burning tree to the next ...

... *RACING* with the flames.
By now they had reached the highest branch of the mango tree.

Koko's nest was about to catch fire!

But Mambi SNATCHED it away in the nick of time!

She carried Koko's whole nest, babies and all,
to the safety of the shady hill, next to the cool green lake.

'Thank you for saving our lives!'
cried Koko, with tears of joy.
'I wish I were as BRAVE as you, Mambi!'

'You're a MARVEL!' trilled Tonga in awe.
'I wish I had your long legs, Mambi.
Then I would JUMP like you!'

Mambi thought about everything that had happened that day.

About flying. And swimming.

About air, and water, and earth.

And about fire.

'Let's not *ever* wish we were someone else,'
Mambi said slowly to her friends.

'Because each of us has a gift
that is very, **very** special.'

Don't YOU think so?

Nandana Dev Sen

Nandana is an award-winning actor, writer and child-rights activist. After studying literature at Harvard, Nandana worked as a book editor, a screenwriter, a poetry translator and as Princess Jasmine in Disneyland. She has starred in over 20 feature films and is also the author of *Kangaroo Kisses* (Otter-Barry Books). Nandana lives in Kolkata, London and New York, and works with children (and grown-ups) at UNICEF, Operation Smile and RAHI to fight against child abuse. She loves to eat, play, bike, dance and argue.

Saskia Pekelharing

Saskia Pekelharing is an illustrator with a love for vibrant colours. Her work is happy, colourful and funny. Her illustrations bring one back into the imaginative world of pretend play and daily discoveries of childhood. Saskia hand-paints all her illustrations. When she is not illustrating, she teaches art to children with special needs. Saskia has lived in the Netherlands, New York and Kenya and has brought a smile to many children's faces all over the world.